PLANT THE TINY SEED

Christie Matheson

Greenwillow Books
An Imprint of HarperCollins*Publishers*

HarperCollins
PUBLISHERS
Since 1817

Plant the Tiny Seed
Copyright © 2017 by Christie Matheson.
All rights reserved. Manufactured in China.
For information address HarperCollins Children's Books,
a division of HarperCollins Publishers,
195 Broadway, New York, NY 10007.
www.harpercollinschildrens.com

Collages were used to prepare the full-color art.
The text type is 30-point Stempel Schneidler.

Library of Congress Cataloging-in-Publication Data is available.

Matheson, Christie, author, illustrator.
ISBN 978-0-06-239339-5 (trade ed.)
"Greenwillow Books."

First Edition
20 21 SCP 10 9 8 7 6 5

 Greenwillow Books

For Vivi

There's magic in this tiny seed.
Press it down
and count to three.

Plant another, then one more.
Press them down
and count to four.

Wiggle your fingers

to add some water.

That's enough.
Next, rub the sun to make it hotter.

Tap the cloud

and wish for rain.

Clap to bring the sun again.

Aaaaaaah!

Find the worm. (Look for its tail.)

Shoo away the hungry snail.

Tell the little bud good night.

Guess what you'll see in the morning light.

Wow!
Now point to the purple flower.

Bzzzzzzzzz!
Tap the cloud again . . .

It's another rain shower!

Touch the blossoms gently, please.

Oooh!
Now jiggle the plants
to scatter the seeds.

The purple flower needs a clip.
Swipe across the stem—snip, snip!

Close your eyes.
Wave your hands in the air.

Oh, look!
There's magic everywhere!

PLANT YOUR OWN TINY SEEDS
Some of the easiest plants to grow from seeds are peas, beans, and zinnias. Zinnias are the flowers in this book!

To grow your own zinnias, you need seeds, soil (that's dirt for growing things), water, and a sunny place. If you grow them inside, you also need a flowerpot big enough for the roots the plant will grow. Roots are the parts of the plant that usually grow under the top layer of soil. They hold plants in place and bring water and food from the soil to the rest of the plant.

If you plant zinnias outside, wait for warm weather and plant the seeds in a spot that gets plenty of sunshine. (Inside, put your flowerpot in the sun, too!) The seeds should be about ¼ inch deep in the soil, three or more inches apart. Water the soil enough to keep it nice and moist but not soaking wet. Little seedlings could sprout in four or five days, and flowers may appear in a few weeks.

Bright, colorful zinnia flowers attract butterflies, hummingbirds, and bees. Bees' favorite flowers are purple, hummingbirds go to red flowers, and butterflies are drawn to lots of bright colors. All of them love zinnia nectar (which is like sweet water), and when they visit flowers, they also spread pollen (powder that helps plants produce seeds). That's very good for the garden!

Worms in the garden loosen the soil, so the plants can get air, water, and nutrients that they need. Snails, however, like to eat leaves. If you see a snail, gently move it away from your zinnias! Ladybugs eat some of the pests that damage plants. Did you find the ladybug in every picture?